BLOOD: Tales of Murder and Fantasy

by

MARCELLE THIÉBAUX

© Thorne River Books, New York, NY 10024

Acknowledgments

My thanks to the valued mentors and critics of my work: crime writers Alison Gaylin, Jonathan Santlofer, S.J. Rozan and fellow members of New York's Crime Fiction Academy; fantasy writer Karen Heuler; and fiction writers Beth Bauman, Gabriel Cohen, Jessica Francis Kane, Victor LaValle, Gabriel Roth, Thaddeus Rutkowski, Mark Spencer.

"The Night of DeLyria" was first published in a different form in August 2013 in *Mondays are Murder* by Akashic Books.

"The Glass Arcade," under another title, was a winner in the Writer's Digest 82nd Annual Writing Competition.

BLOOD: Tales of Murder and Fantasy
Copyright: Thorne River Books
Published: September 2015
ISBN: 978-0-9967058-0-6
Publisher: Thorne River Books

Published by: Thorne River Books, New York, NY 10024

Table of Contents:

For Cam

Guillotine

1

GUILLOTINE

I close my eyes for the kiss of the blade. I arch back and lean on my elbows, straining my body upward in a welcoming curve. My throat is bared to the shining wedge that flashes above me, primed and eager for the descent.

Big razor, come! Such a fine-tuned instrument, the head-chopper, so efficient a means of expediting my exit. A knife's edge that falls seven feet in a single second. Nothing crude about it. The earliest model was the work of a harpsichord craftsman who invented the tall frame, an upright lyre for slaughter.

Swat! Slice! My head leaps up, spurting strings of gore and dropping backward into its appointed basket. Already, blood drains into my throat and I can taste it, coppery at the root of my tongue. My long, black hair streams like a comet. My severed head wallows in the basket, flails and flops and fidgets, my eyes still rolling. My gnashing teeth grind, bite at the bottom of the hamper. Wrecking the wicker. The wear and tear on these head baskets can be frightful.

Afterward, the steel jaw shines red and dripping. Sated like the crocodile's after a successful dinner. Afterward, my jailers reattach my head to prepare me for my lover. They tie it back on my neck with red velvet ribbons, diamond-studded. They have to sheathe my throat with ribbons to keep the two parts of my body together. This way the cut won't show. They stick a cigarette between my reddened lips and give me a light.

With the scarlet ribbons, no one would ever guess my head had been cut off. With the cigarette dangling between my sanguinary lips, I moan and snivel a couple of bluesy cabaret ditties. "Blood Tango." "Dream a Little Blood of Me."

My executioner, my love, comes by night, having completed his job of pulling the lever to release his majestic blade on me. "Alyssa," he tells me, "how beautiful you are." He's in formal attire, my musical cabaret hero. Lyrics on his carmined lips for an evening of love and light opera. Umbrella over one arm. "In case our night of love should prove too rainy with a red lavender downpour," he says.

He's natty in a white tie, and his gloves are swank. Maybe he's a little drunk. He brings me a bouquet of roses. *Blood-red roses tell you of joy*, as the song goes. He takes me in his arms and we begin our love dance. Smiling and handsome in a black mask, tights sleeked to the hips, his codpiece distended and enticing inside the tights. Full, ripe, and pulsing. Forearms bulging, he looks competently robust. Hard. Endless night with him will be hot, sensual, blissful in this desirable dream world of the dead.

THE NIGHT OF DELYRIA

The night before Christmas 1937, the taxi dancer calling herself DeLyria was murdered in the bath
of a luxury park-view apartment.

The Gardenia
Friends last saw her at midnight when she left
the Gardenia Dance Hall on Central Avenue. Her
guys and gents waited outside in the slush. Their
wallets bulged, their hearts swelled.
"Hey, DeLyria, I got paid!"
"How about dinner and champagne at the
Ritz!"
"Marry me, DeLyria!"
Stepping downstairs, DeLyria showed herself.
Platinum strappy dance shoes peeping from open
galoshes.   Dimpled   silk-stockinged   knees,
twirly-hipped skirt, monkey-fur jacket dyed
heavenly blue. Her face of an odalisque gladdened
her groaning fans. They adored her plummy
Flame-Glo lips and her tiny chocolate drop of a

beauty mark. The dark spit curl pasted to her forehead. The yellow felt hat clamped to her head like half a lemon.

She smiled, brandishing glossy, oversized teeth.

"Sorry, fellas," she flung at the fans. "I got a heavy date!"

Among the crowd, watchful and meditative, muffled in an old brown scarf, stood the elderly podiatrist Dr. Ludwig Scherpe. He sized her up, this dancer, how she minced and tottered in the open flapping overshoes, kicking at the fallen snow. A big girl, but not too big. He would advise his boss how to do it. The bathtub would be best. Then a suitcase, a very large suitcase with a leather strap.

The Bath

Her lover slugs her, and her neck snaps. He seizes both her hands in one of his and hits her again, his gold signet ring catching her jaw. She's had a lot to drink and she shrieks, in shock. "Hey you! You! What are you doing?" His next blow catches her throat, deadening her gullet. The blow stuns her. She feels herself falling into the full tub, into the bubbly, patchouli-fragrant water. She drops heavily, managing to grunt, "I'm calling the police, the cops're gonna—" Laughing, he punches her across the mouth and she knows the crack of roots, the breaking of front teeth. "My teeth, look what you did to my teeth." She thinks she's spoken these words, but they are only mumbled through bloodied lips. She is strong, but her lover is stronger and he's holding her down. Her gorge gagging, her heart bucking. Her brain floods with a brilliance sharper than the ball of splintered mirrors, turning, turning, in the spangled ceiling of the Gardenia Dance Hall, where she would love to be right now.

Her struggle to live is fierce. She tells herself she can fight, she can claw and brawl, she can yell for her Ma, but her body is numb, helpless, and much is wrong with her arms and neck.

She is lost in the creamy water. A sharp scalpel of pain punctures her eyeballs. In this sloppy sea without a bottom, she can see only her lover's gray, hateful face, now just a smear on the other side of the water. He is intent, muscular, more powerful than God.

The water thickens, grows solid as a goose-feather pillow. She's swilling and swallowing bathwater up her poor nose, into her lungs. Her lungs are sponging water hard as cement, and she is getting locked up inside this solid gray cement water.

Before her eyes turn to milk-glass marbles, she knows she isn't going anywhere. There's a last bewildered word she tries to murmur, a word like "Why?" She can't utter it and it comes out bubbles, growing flatter, then leveling to perfect stillness.

The Marsh

A black night or two later, when Christmas was over and done with, Dr. Ludwig Scherpe drove into New Jersey's Kearny Marsh, a quagmire known as the Meadowlands. The city slaughter yards had once been there, the marsh full of stinks and the terrified cries of beasts. Now the Meadowlands proved a convenient dumping ground for corpses and old automobile parts. Dr. Scherpe had been charged with getting rid of a body, that of the dancer from the Gardenia.

She was a big girl, bigger than Scherpe, with his short, stocky, stubby-limbed body. Hard to heft. He'd wrestled the suitcase out of his trunk, where it had lain since Saturday night, and dragged her the way she was, wrapped in a blanket and in burlap secured with twine. This dance-hall chippie. No family to speak of, she would not be missed. Yes, yes, he'd seen her when she was full of sluttishness, a big trollopy girl swaying on those high heels of hers, rocking those female hips. He'd had no inclination for her. He didn't like women.

He had chosen a spot where the reeds were thickest, farther out than the morass where they dumped the trash and rusted fenders. Out here in different seasons the black herons, the moor hens and pied-billed grebes would take over. Mosquitoes big as rats would suck your blood. Prehistoric oyster shells from the time when the Jersey Meadowlands lay under the ocean. Blue crabs and who knew what else. He'd brought a pick and the short shovel. He dug, breaking up the hard winter sludge until his back muscles burned. He was no youngster, but he dared not stop to rest. Only the scrape of the shovel blade broke the silence.

After throwing her in, he did what he had to, pulling off part of the blanket, bringing the shovel down on the upturned face, smashing it again and again until her beauty was a dark pulp, as cold as the red snow beneath. Panting, he drove straight down with the edge, spading furrows into eyes, nose, and teeth, as if he were spading the earth for potatoes. Her own mother wouldn't know her. His breath came short and thick, and as he did this duty he felt tremendous rage against the dead *hure*, a rage he could not explain. She'd known what she was doing, she had meddled free and easy with a gentleman out of her class. For a time Scherpe worked steadily to fill in the pit. Just once, his nausea nearly got him, but he swallowed to force the bile to stay put. No getting sick over this. He had his orders, and she'd had it coming. Blood spattered his raincoat; scraps of tissue and bone hit his glasses. Stoically he went on. These were his orders. *Befehl ist Befehl.* An order is an order. Once in her crimson bed, she'd stay down there a good long while.

His work done, Dr. Scherpe steered his battered Ford out of the marsh along Malinski Street. It was a desolate dirt road, unlit except by his headlights. On both sides grew slender reeds, gracefully bent with pure snow. Checking his rearview mirror, the driver saw nothing of importance. *Alles in ordnung*, his father used to say. Everything in good order. No nosy-bodies following.

In the mirror, the doctor glimpsed his own small blue eyes filmed like clouded blueberries, watery and bloodshot behind the glint of his spectacles. The rimless lenses were spattered with soil and blood, but he could not wipe them while he was driving. He swerved past mounded snow toward the Passaic River, then to the Belleville Pike. He hooked back onto Fish House Road with its boarded-up shacks and finally made for the Pulaski Skyway.

No traffic. He was alone. From the Skyway he saw the all-night fires spewing from smokestacks that never rested, staining the night air a lovely yellowy pink. The tireless flashing sign, *Kopper's Coke.* The white Colgate factory, a large cube on his right. Up ahead, the sharp lights of Secaucus, Weehawken, Kearny, Hudson City, and Jersey City twinkled like Christmas. His mother had done that at home, dressed a Yuletide tree with candles. He reached a pudgy hand under the seat for his Pepto-

Bismol, unscrewed the cap by holding the pink bottle against his barrel chest, and took a good swallow. Hangover, indigestion, diarrhea—that's what they advertised on the label. Not what he'd been doing. He screwed the cap back on and threw the bottle under the seat. He wore a cheap porkpie hat and, over the secondhand overcoat, a dirty trenchcoat, all purchased from the Yorkville *Heilesarmee*—the Salvation Army. Such items as he never wore, and would right away discard.

Up here on the Skyway, he saw again in his fevered mind's eye the long, brown, whispering grasses and cattails—"punks," they called them as kids, and smoked them when he was growing up on the East Side of New York City in the Yorkville section of "Germantown." He saw the swamp, the ice-filmed puddles, the muck and slush of the Hackensack Meadows where he had stuffed the *hure*. Packed her down as deep as he was able to dig.

He reached the Holland Tunnel, a mile and a half of hard-gleaming white tile, like a toilet. He drove through to downtown Manhattan. From there he took the car north and over to Yorkville. Here he had lived all his life. His tensed, bunched-up shoulders eased, but as soon as his breathing seemed to return to normal, he nearly cried out with the memory of what he had just gone through.

Dr. Scherpe drove until the sun reddened from

the East Side of Manhattan. Sun bounced off his dirty spectacles. His eyes were gravelly from a night without sleep. Back at last in his modest rooms—salon, kitchen, bathroom and bedroom—adjacent to his Podiatry Parlors, he felt the welcome relief of home.

The Podiatry Parlors

His office and rooms commanded a third-storey bow window at the corner of Lexington and Eighty-Sixth Street near Schaller & Weber delicatessen, where the doctor was a respected patron. The raincoat and cap he had already rolled and dropped off the bridge into the Hackensack River.

Here in his surgery and consulting rooms, the doctor tended the bunions, hammer-toes and corns of the Teutonic feet of Yorkville. Retiring to his tiny, sterile bathroom, the doctor bathed and shaved. He rinsed his spectacles with alcohol. He powdered his forehead and cheeks with white talcum and refreshed himself with Muhlens 4711 cologne. His bed was heaped with featherbeds where he could have thrown himself down and slept for a month.

He put on a Berlin tailored three-piece wool suit, and knotted a cravat of silk. Appraised himself in the armoire mirror. Cloud of fluffed silver hair, baby-soft jowls, budlike mouth—all passed inspection. *Alles in ordnung.*

Tucking a spotless kitchen towel in his collar, he set a pot on the stove of his kitchen to brew strong coffee. With three aspirins, he drank his coffee standing and wolfed down two or three day-old rolls. His thighs ached. There was a fierce, tight pain of the neck and shoulders, a scratchiness of the eyelids. If he closed his eyes for a moment, he saw the road, the reeds, the marsh. If he kept them closed longer, he saw what he did not wish to see.

He stepped into the sanctum of his surgery, immaculate, pungent with antiseptic. He inspected his foot charts: talus to phalanges, hallux, metatarsal. They soothed him. He checked the peephole in the wall behind his diploma from the Long Island Medical College, *anno domini* 1911. Three ladies sat quietly in his waiting room. The doctor donned a pure white coat over his suit. Before seeing his nine o'clock patient he made a call, speaking low into the mouthpiece of his black columnar phone apparatus.

"The pharmaceuticals are delivered, *mein Herr*." As he hung up, he again beheld the marsh, the snow, the wrapped bundle. He saw the blue simian pelt, the monkey-fur jacket that, unearthed, was swimming upward in the coming spring rains to lodge among the cattails. A rheumatoid trembling assailed the doctor's legs. Leaning against the wall, he violently quelled the spasm.

He opened the door to the waiting room, where

his nine o'clock patient waited. In his surgery he bowed and correctly kissed her hand, his lips just grazing and not really touching her skin. He requested her to remove her shoes and stockings. Once they were seated, Dr. Scherpe cradled in pink, comfortably cushioned palms, his first foot of the day.

THE GLASS ARCADE

The death toll soared in the hot summer of 1933. Berlin newspapers published the names in the daily death chronicle, with no explanation of how they died.

Storm troopers did the killing. They slew the slackers and scoffers, defeatists, Poles, Jews, cabaret wits, gypsies, pansies, and onlookers who didn't salute. Storm troopers wore uniforms of brown and marched up and down the avenues in disciplined columns, singing in time with the rhythmic tramping of their jackboots.

Berliners at home called it a brown shitstorm, once they turned up the radio to muffle their words.

Days and nights were sultry. Everyone sweated, oppressed by fear and the battering heat. The first week in August, a full moon burned like a spotty orange and the foliage hung limp as tongues from the acacia trees along Schierkerstrasse.

Six men set out for work. They belonged to a

gang that called itself the Neighborhood Self-Defense Team—old soldiers joined by the jobless and some cops, electricians, and plumbers who kept themselves fighting fit by beating up whoever deserved it. Tonight they had a personal mission: to bludgeon the Pole who was fucking Eckert von Reinmar's sister.

The men of the Neighborhood Self-Defense Team ran up the five flights of the Pole's tenement building on Schierkerstrasse. They carried hammers, and billiard cues from the Nineveh Café, the local storm troopers' pub where they drank, bragged, and bunked down. They were all brothers-in-arms, and Reinmar was their war-crippled buddy. They were out to teach the Pole a lesson.

Reinmar waited in the weedy courtyard below, with the chained bicycles and trash bins. He was the lookout. He was aggrieved, and he was righteously pissed, this wounded old campaigner from the Big War. He was thirty-two years old. The poison taste of his hatred for his sister filmed the back of his tongue; it scalded his throat; it threatened to cut off his breathing. Once, Cristel had lived for him alone, her hero brother Eckert. She was pliant, meek and respectable, a trusted secretary working for the Reichs Ministry on the Bendler Block to support the two of them. They were strapped. Couldn't make it on his lieutenant's pension. He depended on her. She paid for his

schnapps and his hookers. On weekends she was a
home-abiding girl, cooking his meals, ironing,
cleaning, mending his shirts. That was then.

All of it changed. She met this man, this Pole,
and she dishonored the family. A Pole was as good
as a degenerate, a criminal type, an enemy of the
Reich. It was clear to Eckert that this dark, cross-
eyed, greasy villain was her lover.

Reinmar had followed them and publicly
accused the two where they sat drinking together
in the glassed-in arcades on Marburgerstrasse. The
arcades were high and ornate, all swooping
cathedral arches. Beneath the glass arcades, the
gray sky threw an eerie subaqueous twilight on the
guilty pair. The scene infuriated him.

His sister raised her pale, frightened eyes to
Eckert's. She'd had her hair newly waved, tinted a
treacherous red. Her thin frock obviously cost
money and she wore a gold chain. She had taken to
powdering her face. He'd seen the "mystic pow-
der" she carried in a silver vanity compact, and he
knew she ordered it specially. Did she think she
was Hollywood? Did she think she could get away
with this brazen back-stabbing? In a righteous fury,
Eckert had stumped into the arcade on his cane, the
crutch under his other arm. Cane and crutch were
pretty good weapons, but his wooden arm was
better.

"What you do with him stinks all over you!" he

shouted. To hide his ruined face, Reinmar habitual-ly wore a cloth mask looped over the ears. A brown moustache was painted on it. Above the mask his fine gray eyes blazed with a demented rage. He banged the cane on the table. A goblet shivered and spilled. A chair overturned. Cristel screamed.

The Polish fellow's spectacles dropped when he sprang to grab Eckert's swinging arm. This lowlife Pole, this Darius Wyk, dared to lay a hand on Reinmar and shove him away from Cristel. But he hadn't kept Reinmar from slashing her face with his heavy wooden arm. He would have dealt her a second chop, but she fell to the table like a broken doll. It was his old reliable wooden arm that clubbed her. *Let her taste it!* Reinmar liked it much better than the lightweight aluminum prosthesis Cristel had bought for him, and which he found worthless as a weapon.

While Reinmar stewed in the courtyard, his buddies were busy upstairs in the Schierkerstrasse flat. One trooper pitched his shoulder against Darius Wyk's door. Another man gave it a boot and they were in. A flashlight swept over a lumpy bed and a tilting dresser, a pitiful bookshelf, and in the corner a stinking *klo*. What *dreck*, the trooper in charge told his men. Anybody who slept with the windows shut didn't deserve to live.

The killing went on for fifteen minutes.

Wyk struggled in the grip of a suffocating

dream. He believed he was sinking in quicksand. He awoke in a panic. Two men grabbed his arms as he tried to reach under his pillow for his revolver. Too quick for him, they seized it and threw it across the room. One hit him in the mouth to stop his cry, while the other wrenched his arm from its socket.

In the dimness Wyk saw the drab sheen of metal, of buckles and uniform buttons. He did not recognize the men but he knew who they were and why they were here. He understood that all was over for him. Filled with anguish, his death fully understood, Wyk protested that he loved the woman and would marry her, that he had not dishonored her. He had never committed an injury against her brother.

The men pulled him to the floor. His head hit a table corner. He felt the first blow that crushed the back of his neck. Boot heels rained down on his body, and he cried out in agony before they drove pool cues into his eyes and left him in a pool of his blood.

Noises stirred in the building, and neighbors awoke to hammer on the walls and complain about the racket. In the streets below, police cars, fire trucks, and ambulances of Berlin's night security forces roared about their clamorous business as usual, unaware of the bloodstained drama on the fifth floor of the Schierkerstrasse tenement.

The comrades ran down the stairs. In the yard, they thumped Reinmar on the back with a triumphant yell. They all piled into a waiting van and drove back to the Nineveh Café to blow off steam and drink until dawn. Thirsty and exultant, they had much to cheer about. They rehashed the night's good work and regaled all who would listen with how they had punished the Polish scum who'd had the effrontery to soil a German girl. Reinmar drank in every detail. He wanted to hear the story recounted many times over, never tiring of hearing how they broke the Pole.

♦

Oddzial II, the Polish intelligence division, lay buried deep inside the Polish consulate on Kurfürstenstrasse.

Commander Michals, chief of Oddzial II, read the reports on the murder of his operative Darius Wyk. A German war veteran named Eckert von Reinmar had fomented the incident. It looked like a crime of sexual vengeance. The Self-Defense gang had not apparently spotted Wyk as a Polish spy, but Michals decided the operation was compromised and would have to be scrapped.

Wyk, scholarly and bespectacled, had gleaned reliable statistics on Report 4. German troops were moving to military camps in the Vinnytsa zone of Ukraine to rearm. German pilots were training to fly Russian planes. Ukrainian plants turned out fleets of tanks and armored trucks called "sports cars." Germany and Russia were planning a war. The first killing ground of this imminent war would be Poland.

Typed carbons of Report 4 had been coming from a mousy German secretary in the Reichs Ministry, the girlfriend of Darius Wyk.

To take care of immediate business, Commander Michals called in a female agent. She was Olga Onufro, a woman proud of her family name and claiming hereditary kinship with an ascetic of the early Egyptian desert, the holy monk Onufrius. Built solid as a man and endowed with coldblooded capabilities, Olga Onufro was expert at disguises. A fluent linguist, she spoke perfect German.

Commander Michals decided the Self-Defense gang had to be swiftly, methodically picked off, beginning with Eckert von Reinmar.

He assigned Agent Onufro to Reinmar. She put together a scheme to seduce Reinmar, who would be found accidentally floating in the Landwehr Canal. Just about where the headless corpse of Polish patriot Rosa Luxembourg had been thrown a decade earlier.

♦

Leaning on his cane, Eckert von Reinmar labored at a good clip down Tauentzienstrasse. He mopped his neck with a damp handkerchief. Another sweltering August night. He was in a shopping neighborhood from which the Jewish owners were being evicted—and about time, reflected Reinmar. But the windows of the grandiose "department store of the West," the Kaufhaus des Westens, or Ka-de-We, still flaunted silks in the shimmering hues of an oriental bazaar. Placards blazoned foreign names: *crêpe madeleine, crêpe gitta, crêpe musamba, crêpe niumiga.* Women would know all about these alien stuffs that were like the draperies of a harem, thought Reinmar, but what women except whores could afford them? Whores like his sister. He had found her out, her new stylish clothes, her improved looks. She was spending money well beyond her meager salary at the Reichs Ministry. Obviously the lover was paying her. Reinmar smiled bitterly to himself beneath the handsome painted mask that shielded his mangled face. He and his Self-Defense comrades had put a stop to that without having to kill the whore his sister had become. She could still go back to work and support him.

Reinmar felt the armies of women out in force today in the streets, saleable women with varnished cheeks and eyes that were painted pools of hunger. The pavement was busy with women on the prowl, sizing up their *kavaliers.* They swirled in eddies, leaned against kiosks and lampposts. They touched the men, intimately. Lips moistly parted, eyes glassy with belladonna, women took Reinmar's arm and brushed against him, but he limped on, impatient in the darkening neon-lit streets. More women than ever laid a gloved hand, sometimes a darned glove, on his good arm or his bad, it didn't matter. They sank their gaze into his, they whispered lascivious promises, offering themselves for the price of a brandy, a needle and thread, a smoke.

One took hold of him more insistently. A black-haired Madonna pressed close, her scented breath on him. Through the lace of her veil, her dark-lashed eyes pierced his own, sharp as a gunshot. Swathed in black, she was a "widow," a prostitute who might have lost her man in the war and was now driven to the streets, or who might have been only dressing the part, as many women did. Wearing the weeds of the bereft, all women languished with desire. She might have said his name, "Eckert," her bloodless lips barely moving, and he felt a shock of lust. He kept going, and realized he wanted her.

He thought of trying to lose her and edged down to Fasanenstrasse. Here were the lesbian saloons haunted by women in cravats and tuxedos, who at dusk could be seen dancing cheek to cheek to the decadent rhythms of Negro music. Reinmar reflected with grim joy that these perverts would soon be dragged to the "wild camps," the torture depots set up all over the city.

He pushed against the hordes. People barged into one another. Uniformed storm troopers shunted pedestrians off the sidewalks into the gutters, laughing with the pleasure of their power.

Again he saw the woman coming at him, the black-veiled widowed Madonna. She must have followed him, limping like him, and dug her finger in the flesh of his arm. This time he didn't shake her off.

"I've broken the heel of my shoe." Her voice was hoarse and throaty. "Help me to walk, Lieutenant von Reinmar."

He stopped. The filigree veiling set off the dead pallor of her face, fleshy and coarse-featured, not young.

"Do I know you?" he asked.

She bowed her head. "You should," she cryptically answered.

He stared at her. Who was she? If he'd ever seen her before, he would have remembered this woman, but the plush dots and arabesques of her veil put him off. Like his own, her face was half-masked. "How do you know my name?"

With a shrewd smile, she held his wooden arm for support. She lifted her black calf-length skirt so he could study her burgundy-stockinged ankle. It was thick and not at all graceful. She wore heeled shoes of dark red lizard.

"I was wrong. It isn't broken after all." She

smiled.

He bowed curtly, and disengaged her hand from his prosthetic arm. "Then please excuse me!"

"Eckert, wait. I have information for you."

He regarded her with suspicion. Like the heel, it was a ruse.

"What do you want?" he demanded. They were standing near a short flight of stone steps. The door at the top was painted a scaling dirty blue.

Gramophone music poured from a nearby cabaret. *Ich bin ein Vamp! Ich saug die Männer an und aus.* "I'm a vamp, I suck men in and out!" A poster read *Isst Greta Garbo Käse?* "Does Greta Garbo eat cheese?" Reinmar shot a distracted look at it.

"Please!" The black Madonna pointed to the peeling blue door behind her. "We can talk more easily in here."

He had no idea how he'd walked into such a trap when he thought he was rambling aimlessly, and yet here they were beside a door she wanted him to enter. She knew where they were.

The woman said, "I have a key." Her voice wasn't refined, but a gruff contralto. A man? Reinmar examined her cheeks for signs of a shaved, powdered beard but they were silken and doughy. He panted to go with her, though this didn't feel like a usual street pickup. It might have been planned, and he ought to be wary. But his senses were aroused as she leaned on him with her warm, heavy body.

He read the list of offices, each with its buzzer. Physicians treated ailments from neuroses to constipation. Reinmar ran an eye down the list: excitability, sleeplessness, nervous depressions, headaches, tremors, digestive disorders, fatigue, sexual neurasthenia. Sick, sick, the whole city was sick, and here were the cures. Eckert was familiar with every kind of clinic. He felt at home in them— indeed, he rather liked them. He followed her inside.

He checked the empty hall with its scrubbed tiled floors. A few light bulbs were blown out. He threw the woman against the wall in a rough move to assert his control. "Who are you?"

"I'll tell you everything you want to know. Quick, before anybody sees us." He felt the powerful sexual charge between them.

He weighed the situation. He had his weapon strapped inside his jacket. He could take his chances. He would shoot her in the face before she got away with anything. He followed her through a maze of white hallways lined with doors. *Private sanatorium. Hygienic clinic. Hormonal injections.*

"Here." She stopped at a door. He read the engraved brass plaque: *Professor Doktor of Medicine Frau Clara Steengraf. Hydrotherapy. Electrical, Mineral, Compressed Air Baths. Treatments for Male and Female Neurasthenia. Grunewald and Berlin.*

He tore the widow's veil from her heavy, heart-shaped face, revealing an overripe beauty, exotic and sultry. She might be an actress, an aging diva from a derelict theater.

"Who is Frau Doktor Steengraf? Not you!"

"I work for the Frau Doktor. She's at the Grunewald clinic for two days. We'll be alone in here." She unlocked the door, drawing him inside and relocking it. She snapped on lights, illuminating an alabaster office. Pink fluorescence coldly fell from ceiling bulbs. There were hovering carbolic and iodochloric odors that he found intensely exciting.

Wall cabinets latched with morgue-like metal handles furnished the place. On one side stood a high rectangular glass tank in which a patient might stand or tread while submitting to an electrical water bath. The tank was like a glass-sided coffin. A sarcophagus of glass. *Der gläserne sarg.* He remembered folk tales of overlong slumbers in such coffins where sleepers lay entombed until the lid could be pried loose with a crowbar, smashed with mallet and pickaxed to let in the sky.

"What's this all about?" he put it to her, and grabbed her face in both hands, his thumbs on her white lips. She opened her mouth with sly piquancy, showing the redness of her tongue, the lining of her oral membranes like a snake's. He let her go.

"It's a clinic for neurasthenics," she said.

"That's not what I'm asking you. You, what are you all about?"

"You'll see. There's a message."

"Well, move faster. Isn't there any heat in here?"

"It's coming up in a minute," she said.

She removed the veiled hat. He looked her over, the black hair in thick knots, the hoop earrings, the jowled, heavy face. She took off her fur coat. Under it was a jacket embroidered in byzantine colors of maroon, purple, russet. She was outlandish. She hadn't yet asked for money.

"Where do you come from in that getup?" he demanded.

"*Stambul*," she said, offhandedly. "I work for the Türkei Konsortium of the Deutsche Bank. The Berlin–Baghdad Railway sector.

Reinmar stared. "You look ridiculous." But he was electrified.

"I have a few wardrobes. When I work in the clinic, I wear white as a hygienic measure. Uniform, shoes, and stockings. Would you like to see me in a white coif? I'm a nursing sister."

"Don't bother. I know the game." The game was nothing original. The nurse in her role as *kokotte*, clinically ministering to her patient under the bed linen. The thought inflamed him, even as it made him dislike her. He mistrusted her foreign look. "Never mind. The way you are. Hurry up, it's cold in here."

"If you want," she said with an oily smile, "I can give you something. We can *injizieren*. An injection to make us feel good. Gratis. More pleasurable that way. Let's lie down in a cubicle."

He looked at the walls of the boxed-in cubicle. Photos of patients before and after treatment by Doktor Steengraf showed withered limbs, bodies stippled with eczema, made magically whole.

"What's the injection?" Her smell was pungent, myrrh and patchouli overlaid with the antiseptics. Reinmar was on fire.

"It will be good, don't worry." She opened a cabinet crammed with hypodermics, flasks, rubber bladders with nozzles attached.

"You first," he told her.

She coyly smiled and pushed up her left sleeve, bared her arm, tied it with rubber tubing, and filled a syringe. He watched closely, seeing the syringe go in her arm.

On an impulse he took out his weapon, cocked it, and shoved the barrel in her mouth while she injected herself. He liked seeing her gag, convulse. Her eyes flew wide open, and she choked until he withdrew the barrel. It came out smeared wet with her saliva.

"Wipe it off," he ordered. She bent her head and used a clean towel. She seemed to recover as if nothing had happened. "Shall I take your arm?" She refilled the syringe.

He yielded his good arm to the syringe, feeling barely a prick as it skillfully entered a vein. After a numbed lull, he felt cold.

He heard her say from a distance, "You will be fine." He saw her put on her coat. She stuffed the black-widow veil in her bag.

"Where are you going?"

"I have errands. Your sister says hello." Her voice was hoarse, unfurling like fog from a grotto.

"My sister!" He felt colder than he ever thought possible. "Who are you?" Alarmed, he tried to rise but nothing in his ruined body worked. His lungs were frozen sacs.

"Darius Wyk sends greetings. You'll have a chance to meet him. Get to know each other." She picked up her gloves and purse. The lines of her face blurred, deliquesced, thawed. A woman of snow.

He felt his mouth fill with choking snow. The room's white cold coagulated the blood in his chest. Breath refused to enter his body. His heart strained in terror.

A wintry weight stifled his chest and he lay under an avalanche. His muscles would not move. Heart bursting in a frigid panic, he fought to get up but could only lie congealing in a glacier's nightmare. He felt his brain trepanned, anesthetized in a doctor's snow-packed surgery. His larynx throttled with cotton slush. He snatched off the cloth mask for air, but it didn't help. He stopped breathing, he was in the bondage of a prehistoric ice age, and this was among his last thoughts as he stared through panes of iced glass, pressed against his face, reddened with his blood. He was trapped in the glass coffin, lying beneath an arcade so low that the glass roof splintered and ground fragments into his face, his naked brain. People were dragging his glass coffin through the streets. He tried seeing through the clear lid, looking for his sister. Where was Cristel? "My sister, where is my sister?" The street narrowed to an alley sloping to a nether realm of ice. He felt nothing but the lid of the glass coffin, pressing against his bleeding brain.

♦

Olga Onufro walked to the reception. She opened the clinic door to admit the two men who waited outside. "Room Seven," she murmured with her dark smile of a desert sphinx. She slid past them and made her way from the building to the hot sooty pavement.

RUE RAVENDER'S BLOOD WEDDING

For a long time Rue Ravender has known that a demon spirit dwells on the far side of her mirror. She's felt his presence, and now she wants to entice him to come out, persuade him, drag him from that glassy abyss where he's imprisoned.

Desperately, Rue needs an ally. The mirror demon could help her get free of her grandmother's cruel clutches. She'd help him, too, for she's sure he longs to escape his own bondage.

She's got to concentrate, fix her attention on him by candle or moonlight. She knows how to discover secrets of the past and future by scrying in a shining surface. She can scry in a saucer of clear water, a crystal or crystal ball, even an ink drop or a puddle after the rain. But she likes her mirror, since she can look at herself at the same time. She loves to preen and primp, examine her own face— pale, intense, eyes staring, her wild hair yellow and tangly.

She peers into the glass of her bedroom vanity.

She tries calling him. "I need you, please, please come."

All at once a breathing cloud rises within the mirror's core. A silver shadow forms a man's countenance. Stunned, Rue sees her own reflected features dissolve. Glimmering through the mist, the mirror demon appears, faint as a scent. His half-closed eyelids are still, his brow harsh, but he is beautiful. His severe mouth barely moves. Rue sinks to the cushioned hassock before her vanity mirror, the blood banging in her temples. She's terrified, entranced.

"Speak to me," whispers the mirror's muffled voice. "I've waited so long."

In a bizarre language that Rue strangely grasps though she's never heard it before, the demon makes her understand he's trapped in a galaxy of deathless stars. In eternity, without past, present or future, he is congealed in pure stasis, in emotionless, unchanging existence. But he's seized on her summons and it has stirred feelings in him, the first and only feelings he's ever known.

"Your summons," he says, "has roused in me a desire for human consciousness. To be with you, and to be yours."

Rue gasps, astonished. Can she understand this? Yes, she can. She is thrilled by his voice, and the fact that she's called up this apparition by herself.

"Yes, you must. My dear one." She doesn't know what to call him. He looks like a man. Is he a man?

The feeling he describes, oh yes, she knows it. She herself is trapped in this heavily guarded hellhole of her grandmother's Hudson Boulevard house, where the girls live in enslavement. Forced to yield up their tender bodies to any paying customer the grandmother brings in. Rue has struggled to flee, to save herself, and so far it hasn't worked. This time it looks as if she's found a way— a start, anyhow—by drawing her demon out of the mirror. But can he conjure the necessary force to come to her? From his star-jammed galactic frontier, so far from where she lives, all the way down here to Chemical City?

Once he has told her of his dwelling place and his desire to escape earthward to her, he vanishes as suddenly as he appeared. "No, no!" Vainly she raps on the cold glass, although this is not how scrying is done.

"You've *got* to come back!" Excited, Rue leans right into the mirror. "Tell me who you are. You can see I got you to come to me, and now I want you. I'll be here tomorrow, waiting. Don't fail me!"

The next night the mirror demon returns, and as he shows himself more often, Rue practices shallow breathing so she can draw in his spirit messages. She communicates her own. Already they feel powerfully bound in an affinity like love, although he has yet to learn what exactly love is.

"My beloved mortal girl," he says in that otherworldly star language. "I suppose I can say it, but I'll have to come to you to learn human love."

"I can teach you. Whatever you want, I'll do it." This is a rash promise. She's ready to pledge anything, not knowing what it may be.

He tells her his name, an astral, sky-born name. *Axior*. He longs for a fleshly body of his own when he comes to her so he can fully know her. He can manage to do this for a time right now.

"I have a way of journeying earthward. I can borrow a flesh-and-blood body for my travels. I'll trick my father into arranging a violent storm." Rue smiles to think her lover can deceive his parent.

"You can do that?" Rue asks, delightedly. "I love it already. I love you, Axior. Once you're with me, you'll become a man."

"I want humanity more than anything,"

"I'm sure of my powers. I lured you from the mirror, didn't I? I knew you must be there, and you were. I can save you and make you mine, and then we'll escape this house for good."

◆

Rue's grandmother, Madame Seraphita, gives herself a pat on the back every day of her greedy, conniving life for putting lovely Rue up for sale.

Despite Rue's bad, sassy temper, she's much in

demand among clients. Madame Seraphita has two other girls in her parlor house for gentlemen. All of them living in this house on Hudson Boulevard in Chemical City, Rue the youngest.

Resourceful Madame Seraphita loves money. She has a good head for business, and she's found this surefire way to rake in pots of cash. Opening her residence as a whorehouse of refinement to the gentlemen of wealth and status. All welcome, as long as they're loaded, and like to spend. It's a business that's netted Seraphita a fortune.

Tonight Seraphita fusses over her girls, making sure they're not upset by the bad weather. A storm has brewed and boiled out there in the black sky. The radio voices can't tell how bad it will get in Chemical City. Already vacation houses on Long Island and along the Jersey shore have been blown out to sea like piles of matchsticks.

Madame Seraphita comforts her girls, her financial investments. Rue is her most alluring asset. But stubborn-willed Rue gives Seraphita grief. She's spiteful, rebellious, perverse and disobedient. Madame has tried everything to control the girl.

Rue flouts Madame Seraphita's authority. She's lazy and doesn't want to work. She sulks, stages tantrums. Wastes time reading romance novels, ruining her eyes and demanding eyeglasses. Says she wants to go to school. Who does she think she

is? In her grandmother's view, Rue doesn't
appreciate her good fortune. Pretty clothes,
beautiful home, exquisite food. She has to be
tamed. Whipping the girl's legs with a leather strap
is the most she can do. If she beats her, she'll spoil
her looks. She tries forcing rough clients on her to
discipline her. But brutality only turned Rue into a
scratching, spitting wildcat.

Tonight is the girls' night off, but who can relax
in this bellowing wind? Two girls are fretful. The
storm rampages. Saplings fly uprooted, slate
shingles explode off the roof like cannonballs.
Shutters bang against every windowpane.

At each jagged lightning streak, Gaby and Lucy
cling to each another, whimpering, "We're going to
die!"

"Oh, shut up, you two," Seraphita snaps. "We
can't die, we've got too much money in the bank!
Stop thinking about yourselves for a change and
worry about the damage to our real estate. The
house is in more danger than you, and worth
more."

Lucy and Gaby sob, not seeing see the logic of
this.

Rue, at the window, smiles to herself so the
others can't see. The sky is like raw gin packed
with ice chips. Hailstones pummel the window.
Now the sky turns ragged black, a witches' brew,
thick, roiling, viscous.

The furious sky doesn't bother Rue. Let all the windows shatter and the house fall in a heap of rubble! She doesn't care. Good riddance. She isn't afraid of getting battered by a few hailstones. She's put up with lots worse since her grandmother started inviting men in to do what they wanted with her. Condemned to this hateful, whoring servitude, Rue secretly knows it's coming to an end.

This storm portends everything good. She and Axior set it up between them. He let her know he could arrange it with his old man. That wrathful, turbulent father of his, inhabiting one of the worst imploding and rocketing novas, proves as bad in his way as Madame Seraphita is in hers. Rue and Axior have shared this information once they quickly learned to express her language silently in the mirror.

Rue scans the sky for her galactic guest, champion, and lover. His coming is a sure thing. *I summoned you, and you're mine. Mine!* They both know this.

◆

Out of the past, out of the nucleus of a raging star, the unearthly guest plunges to planet Earth.

Pitching, diving headlong, he falls for days before hitting down with spine-jolting force. He lies naked and half-dead where he falls in the wreckage of an automobile junkyard and a pig farm in

Secaucus, New Jersey.

He revives to feel the nightshades close in. He understands it's an earthly season, Halloween, when phantoms rise up to walk. He's got to avoid them and not let himself be mistaken for one of them. The storm has let up, but Axior must find refuge from the next storm, which won't be long in coming. He crawls, scraping flesh from his belly, and rouses himself.

The man-guest Axior stands, well-grown and wide-shouldered. He's cosmic spirit with a high metal content, but his body contains a complement of bone and flesh, borrowed for a restricted time for his descent to earth.

He studies his bloodied arms, solidly muscled and knotted with thick blue veins. He looks down at his nakedness. He has a human male's cock, but his body is smashed up from the long fall. He bleeds heavily. Human blood pours from his temple, his neck and throat, his chest and groin. He'll recuperate, but he'll need the girl's help.

He finds he's on a bleak plain. The industrial city limits stretch in ruins, ripped apart by the interplanetary storm. The bridge is down, the girders twisted on broken piers. Little but masonry is left of Secaucus, Weehawken, Hoboken, and Union City. Through the Hackensack plain, the river runs swollen with corpses. Vultures swoop to feast. Human debris tosses in a jumble of mud.

Axior turns from the devastation. He has to climb to the upper city to the girl who draws him to her.

He needs to cover his nakedness if he's going among men and women. He has the chameleon's ability to grow garments to fit his body and allow him to adapt to his surroundings. He extrudes a new shell, clothing himself in black leathers, supple and luxuriant. The boots, leggings, and jacket give him a look of studly chivalry. He's nearly a century ahead of his time, in gear that foreshadows a biker's leathers. A super-typical human male, he'll pass muster.

A black maelstrom of wind whirls on the horizon, funneling straight for the man Axior to suck him up and spit him out. It's the monster storm-father that's out to mutilate and destroy him. The deadly wind howls in his ears. He's hunted, haunted, rain-soaked to the bone. It's his terrible father, who abides eternally out there in the cold asshole of the empyrean.

Axior wanted the storm, but not such a bad one that it would level half a city. His father has orchestrated this intergalactic catastrophe, punishing his son for his renegade flight to earth.

Lacking humanity, Axior has never tasted emotion. Stars endure for eons, burning and cold; they are sheer intelligence without sensation.

But the girl beguiled him from his remote

country of the stars with her mortality. Because of her, he knows what he can become. *She has the blood he needs.* He's got to do it, take on a vampyre's habits to get what he needs.

"Blood," declares the heavenly, terrible father out of his storm cloud. "What a laugh. She'll have to give up her blood to you to give you human life. Bullshit. You can be sure she won't do that. There's no percentage in it for her, ha-ha-ha! You can eat your heart out, loser." The old man's phlegmy derision pelts his son with contempt. Axior has to run. His father drives him hard, armed with fire bolts of patriarchal fury, hell-bent on Axior's destruction.

Axior finds a swift way to the heart of the city, clambering up cliffs and crossing the trestles of the Erie Lackawanna Railway line, pounding on foot through flooded cobbled streets. Many houses are battered. Buses lean hub-deep and awash, stalled on dead tires. Drivers slump drowned in their cars.

An interstellar being, Axior has an instinctive understanding of the world's ways when he needs it. He yanks open car doors, seizing what he finds, wet currency from wallets and briefcases. Knowing its usefulness, he stuffs cash into his breast pocket and keeps running, long, iron-black hair streaming and pasted to his white face, teeth clenched in desperation.

Suddenly he stops. He's caught the smell of the

girl. Nostrils flaring, he scents her through curtains of rain and hail. He drinks in the rain, open-mouthed, even as he breathes her in through the walls of the night and the walls of the house rising up ahead. Her smell seeps through clapboard, mortar, brick and stone, through the rock of the ancient cellar. She drives him to paroxysms of desire. His physical need surges through his body from mouth to throat to belly to groin.

It's the blond smell of a girl in her young prime, a warm scent of female blood and maidenhair, musk-cherries, Tunisian neroli, whitethorn, ozone, and green moss wafted on the salt winds of this newly discovered climate of Earth. He needs to bathe in her earthly blood, the life-giving elixir that can release him from endless, dead, unfeeling immortality.

This is how Axior comes to the house, to Madame Seraphita's high-towered, high-class bordello. The gray Victorian mansion looms on Hudson Boulevard in Chemical City. Around the house, the gardens die. Poisonous weeds choke off their green life. Everything in the yard sickens, even mice, worms, and beetles, whose small bodies rot and then desiccate. The man-guest can see right away that everything in this place is wrong. Everything but the sweet girl Rue.

Axior nears the house, sensing that behind the locked doors there's an armed guard posted who might destroy him. He looks up at the windows and calls to the girl in their familiar language.

"Ask me in! I'm here. I've come for you." In his vampyre guise, he can enter a house only if invited. To the other inhabitants, this demon is an unbidden guest, a fugitive without an appointment. No one wants him. Except for one.

She opens the window a crack. "Come on!" She points down to the stairway. "The iron stairs. The fire escape."

He sees what she means, and laughs. "Yes, that's easy for me, after where I've come from."

"It's where I liked to sit and look for you when it was warm. When it was summer, I watched the sun go down and the stars come out. I listened to the trains at night!"

He can't see her through the slashing downpour of rain, but her secret voice gives him a burst of strength. He gauges the height of the iron staircase. He can grab the bottom rung, chin up, and hike himself to the first step. The rest will be easy. He jumps high. It's a basketball player's lunge, Rue recognizes, and she laughs at how good he is at everything. He takes hold of the bar. In an instant he'll make the iron stair.

Lightning splits the sky. A vicious bolt splinters the weather vanes and topples chimneys. A second bolt strikes the fire escape with a meteor's impact.

Axior feels his father's lightning charge

through his newborn sinews. The excruciating pain deadens his nerves. The power outage that blows out half the city lights paralyzes him. The giant staircase wrenches free of its iron struts and flitch plates. With the grating agony of an arm tugged out of a socket, the fire escape strains away from its moorings and falls to the sidewalk with a crash that rocks the house.

Dashed to the pavement, Axior groans aloud and sinks into near-death.

Rue at the window gapes down in horror at the man below, his limbs snared in tangled coils of iron. What if she's only imagined her powers and she can't revive him?

She has to. She's already compelled him to descend from the farthest fringes of the galaxy. She lured him to surf down the heavens to her. He can't expire. In her arms he'll revive.

"Take hold of the iron," she cries. "Climb up, everything's going to be fine. You'll be safe and whole with me."

Axior hears, and counts on her. Freshly bloodied head to foot, he knows terrible pain for the first time.

He hauls himself upright against the fallen stairway, embracing earthly metal. The iron's energy penetrates him, fusing with his star-body's metallicity. From his birth he has his own allotment of iron, beryllium, lithium, and titanium. Exerting his will, he forces his bones to consolidate.

He makes for the opening gouged in the house by the torn iron stair. He shoulders through the space, walking over broken glass and plaster, and sees a beefy figure coming at him from the darkness. A man's shape, like his own.

Doghead Viggo the bouncer bunks in the coal cellar. It's a day off, so he hasn't been on the alert, but the crashing fire escape woke him. Streaked with coal dust, he rushes up with his flashlight to confront the supernatural visitant.

On glimpsing this huge bleeding man who gives off an uncanny glare, Viggo goes slack-jawed. It's the night of the Halloween freaks, he remembers, and that means the dead are roving. Damaged and bloody, this could be a dead man who's staggered away from a car wreck. But this specter is superhumanly built, with that baleful light coming from him. Looking exactly like a man, he's obviously a lot more than a man.

"Who in the fuck are you, bud?" mutters Viggo the watchdog. "Where you coming from?"

"I've been summoned." Axior's human voice is deep, warm, and resonant. He's using this voice for the first time and it feels strange to him.

"Dumbass fuckin' shit!" Viggo growls in a panic. A warm corpse that's been *summoned*? "Get back, Mac, or I'm gonna shoot."

Axior doesn't move. Viggo whips out a weapon

and fires. Axior steps aside to elude the bullet's trajectory, then drives forward and fells the man with a meteor blow of his fist.

The bouncer jerks back against the wall of the coal cellar and slumps in a senseless heap. Axior eyes the man. He didn't want to kill him, just disable him long enough so he could pass. The man's skull isn't broken, and he's still breathing. Axior picks up the weapon. He studies it. Dark blue steel, a snub-nose .32. He understands its workings and shoves it in his leather jacket along with the cash. He doesn't intend to use the gun, but he reasons that if anyone in this house carries a weapon, he'd better be the one.

He looks down at the dogface bouncer, whose big-jawed muzzle and chin are covered with stubble. Axior touches his own face and finds the beginnings of a beard. He understands. As a man, his beard and hair will grow. He turns out the bouncer's pockets, relieving him of money and cigarettes.

He mounts the inner staircase, inebriated by the girl's lovely odors. Through all the barriers, they waver and change. Sea anemone, linden flowers, green tea, mimosa, and, underneath, always the life-giving magic of her blood. She's the focus of his every impassioned thought and requirement. He follows the dark hallway to a glass-windowed door shrouded by a curtain of lace.

Before going in, he wills the dimming of his body's stellar brightness. In time it will fade. As he joins his body to the mortal girl's and his own mortality takes over, he'll lose this awkward radiance. But now he doesn't want to startle the women of the house.

He knocks. Nothing happens. Having tested his strength with the bouncer, he bursts the door open with ease.

The two girls and a woman sit frozen in candlelight. The hanging Tiffany lamp has blown out. Aghast at the man who appears in their parlor, even Madame can't speak for an instant.

They gawk at this tall being, large, handsome, robustly built. He bleeds from fresh gashes in his head. Blood crusts his neck and blotches his black leather collar. His uncut black hair and gaunt face glisten with the wet of his new life's gore. His slicked clothing runs with rain and blood like a snake's back.

Madame Seraphita rises to confront the intruder. "Stop right there," she orders. She's svelte, slim as a whip in her red kimono. Her square-cut black bob frames a face powdered chalky like a kibuki dancer's.

To Madame, a connoisseur of men, this individual doesn't look civilized. He's filthy and bloody. Certainly he's no big spender. He's a wild man, shedding an eerie dark brilliance. He sets her inner alarms going off, and she doesn't scare easily.

"Excuse me—" he begins. But she cuts him off.

"Out! Get out! Right now! Chop, chop!" She claps her hands.

Axior waits, and manages to look less menacing.

She draws herself up. "No clients on All Hallows. This is a solemn saints' holiday. You'll have to leave."

"Clients? Saints?" Smiling, he doesn't get it right away. He wants to laugh. But in an instant he perceives what the house is about. "Can I find hospitality here until the storm is over? A new one is about to begin."

This puts Madame in a royal pique. She stalks to the phone. "This is no hotel. Whoever you are, the police will deal with you."

"The police will never get here. Your city's under siege because of my father."

She knows now he's dangerous, and reaches for the phone. He can't risk her using it in case someone actually answers and comes after him.

He aims Viggo's revolver, firing a bullet into the rococo instrument. It explodes in a glittering spray of gold and ivory Bakelite. The two girls drop to the floor and crawl under the dining table, clutching each another and crying.

"Forgive me," he says, "for destroying your beautiful apparatus. I'm not going to hurt anyone."

He re-pockets Viggo's gun. "That was only to get your attention. I'd like something to eat."

A young girl appears in the parlor doorway. She wears a long, white muslin dress. Her blond hair springs in tousled curls like a pot of buttercups. Drops and smears of blood spot the purity of her white gown.

Madame's breath hisses sharply inward. She pulls her kimono sash taut around her shapely waist. "Back to your room, you little slut. And shut the door behind you."

The girl doesn't move. "Did you hear me?" croaks Madame Seraphita. "Go! Your nightgown is a mess."

The stranger stares at her. Stupefied from his own loss of blood and driven half mad by her seductive scent, he has to keep from striding across the room and taking her in his arms at once. He'd like to make off with her, into the storm, anywhere in the world. Just a touch of that stained, wrinkled dress would save him. He's in a frenzy, but he uses restraint. He doesn't wish to roil the old lady, who's clearly the girl's jailer and keeper.

The girl in white backs away with a bewitching smile.

"Wait, don't go," he says. "What's your name? Is it Rue?"

From now on they use human speech, not the wordless intelligence of the mystical mirror-demon days.

She backs further into the shadows.

"No, don't. Stay!" he tells her. To the powdered duenna he says, with courtesy, "I told you what I need. Since you've already agreed, more or less, I'll stay with this beauty if she wants me. You can bring our supper. Food, alcohol, wine, brandy. The best fare your house can offer."

Rue smiles. The house is well stocked with booze. She casts a wanton eye on the newcomer and turns in a slow mermaid shimmy, graceful hands out to the side, wriggling her slender hips and shoulders. Axior feels his lust rise, feels he can't live more than a few minutes without this girl in his arms, without joining their two naked bodies and both reaching the summits of ecstasy. But he'll endure, he'll observe the polite customs of the house.

He pulls out an embossed, bloodstained morocco billfold. It came from a stranded car he plundered in a flooded alley. He drops huge clumps of green American dollars on the table.

"This girl—" Madame Seraphita tries not to look at the money. "This girl is *not* available. Come back tomorrow and you can have one of my other lovely girls. Lucy or Gaby, or—"

He laughs. "Thank you, but I've come for her."

"You force me to be plain, my dear young gentleman—"

The sight of his money has turned this barbarian into a dear young gentleman. But *is* he young? Enduring for eons, he knows nothing of the ways of love, but he's become young and vigorous and bursting with sexuality. Saucy Rue sees and feels it. She loves the cut and heft of his body, the energy he gives off. For the first time she wants a man. She wants him.

"You can't have her," finishes the grandmother in a petulant rage. "She is *in her flowers.*"

"Flowers? What sort of quaint archaic nonsense is that!" He sifts through what he knows about this planet. At once he understands. *Flowers* means flowing blood. So much the better. He'll sojourn forever with the sweet blood-flowing girl in white.

"To your room, Rue!" cries Madame Seraphita, in terrible dudgeon.

But the girl won't budge, her eyes wide and blue, debauched and innocent—Axior can't tell which, and if he can't, who can? The room holds its breath, the silvered wallpaper, the Japanese vases on the mahogany sideboard, the Victrola flaring its trumpet like a black petunia, the pitcher of Mamie Taylor cocktails, ginger beer spiked with scotch.

"No," says willful Rue. "I'm taking him." She gives him an impish, lascivious once-over.

"That settles it," he says. "Only her wishes matter." He goes to her. "You'll take me, will you?"

"Okay," she says with a shrug. She looks down

at her skirt. She knows what he wants.

"I won't permit this," cries Madame Seraphita, keeping up her high-hat act. Her tone hardens. "Do as I say, Rue, or believe me, you'll feel the strap!"

She crosses the room to lay into Rue, but Axior bars her path. "You can't mean that you would physically harm this girl!"

Rue's stubbornness is delicious. She smiles at him with a sly upcurving of her lip that excludes everyone in the room. Her smile caresses him intimately. Not taking her eyes from Axior, she defies her grandmother. "I'm not going anywhere without him. I like him."

Axior keeps Madame Seraphita at bay, reaches into his breast pockets for more damp bills, and, finding some big denominations, throws them on the lace tablecloth. "Please take this. It's my worldly fortune."

Madame Seraphita, her gold eye shadow streaky with sweat, flings out her hands in defeat, then scoops up the wet, bloody cash. "Damn devil!" she mutters.

Rue studies the wrecked stranger. He frightens her deliciously, his face gaunt and blood-streaked. He thrilled her, the way he walked into their house with sublime confidence saying what he wanted. And let Seraphita keep in mind, he has a gun. She surely hasn't forgotten that! Even though he's probably too much of a gentleman to brandish it in

Seraphita's face, he's at this very minute got the upper hand.

"I love him, everybody. I love how he shot your new telephone dead," she tells her grandmother. "Anyhow, his wounds need care, and he's got to eat. I'll join him for a late supper. I'm hungry myself."

The girls huddle together. Rue is up to her arrogant tricks.

"Tell Olga to bring us a tray. A good one." She throws that over her shoulder. Taking Axior's hand, she leads him down a black hallway to her room and closes the door.

Candles throw fitful flames in her sweet-smelling bedroom. Axior picks up a grass-green lily, a blown-out bulb of Venetian glass.

"Pretty," he says. "Would you like me to fix it?"

"You can't. There's no electricity."

"I'll try." He blows gently on the lamp, igniting it to a glow with his own fire.

Rue giggles. "I love how you did that. You're real convenient to have around, Axior, my mirror demon and star-traveler."

"There's a little more to it, which I'll have to tell you about." He gazes into her eyes, blue as the day sky. "It's just that I need the bliss of your blood to be fully a man."

Rue shrinks from him. "Wait a sec. I didn't know about this."

"It won't hurt, I promise. It's only like a baptism. No more."

Rue edges farther away. "You sound like a vampyre. Is it true?"

"I suppose that's what I am, or a close relation. I've had to accept the role to be able to come here. I want to take you in my arms and love you sweetly, and I'll tell you about it so we can be better acquainted."

"We're already acquainted."

"Not sufficiently. Come, Rue."

"We haven't had anything to eat."

"Later in the evening."

"You haven't seen my library. Do you like to read?"

"I don't know yet," says Axior. "I never have learned."

"My books are over here, heaped on the bed pillows." Rue, a compulsive reader of mendacious trash, keeps a hodgepodge library. A pop romance called *Queen Quasimodo* sits beside *Tarzan and the Ape Girls* and *The Libidinous Crusader*. The truly shameless romances she hides in her mattress.

"There's time, Rue. We have all the time in the world."

He looks for a place to sit on her white dimity bed among piles of underwear, slippers, and silk stockings. He pushes aside her well-thumbed novels.

"Come to me my darling. Didn't you ask for this? For me to come?"

"And you're here."

"I so much need what you have to give."

Rue sighs. She puts her arms around him, and he draws her between his knees in an embrace. She opens her gown. Her breasts are small, exquisite and voluptuous.

"You can kiss me," she murmurs. "I know I'm supposed to ask what *you* want. Around here, it's what the man wants that counts, but since I invited you, and you're my other worldly guest, I can say all rules are off."

"I'm glad we don't have rules," says Axior. He feels shaken with the violent onset of passionate love. It's as painful as he thinks death must be. He's smitten with this girl whom he's already loved from afar. He feels high-strung, invigorated and dead tired. His injured head and the events of the night are beginning to tell on him. All he wants is to love her and collapse for a few hours. The more human he becomes, the more he craves rest and sleep in her arms. All he wants is the blood wedding that will make them both whole together.

He kisses the warmth of her blond hair, her ears and temples, her shoulder and breast. He breathes in her fragrance. She's a riotous garden and he's in torment.

"Tell me what I need to know about your being

a vampyre," says Rue. "I've got to hear what I'm in for."

"The blood of a maiden—didn't you ever hear what a good thing it is?"

She isn't laughing at this. "First, I hope you don't think I'm a maiden or a virgin, because I'm not. I'm stuck here. I have to sleep with every high roller my grandmother brings me and tells me to be nice to. And about a girl's blood—" She hesitates. "It's supposed to cure a person of leprosy, I've read, but she's got to be killed first and the killer takes a bath in her blood *after* she's killed."

"That's sometimes true," says Axior, "or maybe once was. But you're thinking of Elizabeth Bathory, the notorious fiend who bathed in the blood of six hundred virgins to maintain her beauty. No one will ever try to draw your living blood to cure me. I need only to bathe in your female humanity and become mortal man, with you."

"What's your affliction. I mean, what *are* you sick with?

"Don't you know?"

"No, I don't."

"It's living forever."

Rue is wide-eyed. "That's it?"

"Yes, my dearest Rue, that's it. Heal me with the mortality that runs in your veins, that makes life sweet. Whatever you might think, take it from me. Endless existence without change is unbearable."

"Why is it unbearable?"

"Where I come from, the constellations rain down influence, but we're cold and static. We endure always. Or nearly so, with our monotonous self-absorption."

Rue takes this in and thinks it over. "I see. Sort of."

"Will you take me as I am, then, Rue? With this vampyrism that I'm forced to take on, such as it is?"

"You can love me if you want, but maybe I have to look after you first."

"I'm all right," he lies.

She studies the deep, bloody cut in his head. "Alcohol and cotton. Let me get them from my cabinet, and mercurochrome. Not iodine, it stings more and it's uglier looking." She moves away from him, but his arms tighten around her.

"That can wait." He kisses her mouth with ravenous hunger. "For now, let's join our bodies. It's all that matters."

"Do you think so?" She nervously smiles. "Will we be all right together?"

"Yes." He stands up to strip off his clothing. She thinks of the fiend unfolding his leathern wings and wants to snicker, but she's a little scared. He drops everything on the floor. When he's naked, Rue sees that there are ancient scars on his neck and shoulders, like those on his face, but the rest of his strong, long, muscular body is pale, almost bluish-white. It's the celestial hue of his condition, with black hair on his chest, *v*-ing down to his groin and curling around a strong, standing, seaworthy cock.

"Oh, you're beautiful," she murmurs. "Considering."

"*You* are beautiful, Rue." He feels an adoration he could never have foreseen.

Rue decides she'll be okay. He knows how things are with her, but it doesn't seem to mean anything to him about her being in her red flowers. He wants her anyhow. She does have some trepidation about where this is going. She lets her gown slide to the floor.

She sees how he's taking her predicament as if it's pure joy, and she likes him even more. She revels in the forbiddenness, the promise of messiness to come. She examines the network of bluish veins traceable under the soft part of his forearms, and the bones of his wrist. She feels the same lust for him he seems to have for her.

She strokes the length of his body, ribs and hip bones, tucking her hands in the black bramble patch at the joining of his well-socketed legs. It's a body that's very agreeably rigged, in her opinion. And she has seen a few.

Blood sluices down her thighs, puddling on the

carpet. She's about to lie down, but on the bed pillow sits a demitasse cup, the inside glazed with old coffee.

He picks it up. "Shall I find a place for this? We don't want to knock it over."

She throws the cup and saucer across the room, where it breaks. She pulls him to her.

She lays her right arm on Axior's blood-splashed left shoulder. His neck is sturdy and warm. There's a pulse against the inside of her arm, his or hers, she doesn't know. The room clouds around them and they seem to be the main source of light. His mouth is on her breast, his tongue tasting her nipple, his right hand cupped around her hip. She's out of breath with what's happening.

"This is news," she whispers. "I never was glad about hugging any man. It's all been hard-luck duty up till now."

And up until now, having been ordered, scared into submission, drugged on Mariani wine, marijuana cigarettes, cocaine, and lithium soda pop, she's had to knuckle under to importunate clients like the assistant mayor of Chemical City; the warthog hospital commissioner for Margaret Hague Maternity, where she was born; and Mr. Frydevoo, their rich neighbor in the radio sales business.

Rue shunts aside thoughts of the whole pack of them. Maybe a night of fucking her supernatural visitor will cancel them out. At least she can hope so. "I'm finished with them all," she says happily.

She reaches for his divine root at the forking. Breathes the delicious black roughage of his armpits. Isn't it all different tonight, this invited unearthly guest, a fugitive with bleeding scars that honeycomb his handsome body? This man of her choosing? The cramping of her womb and the bubbling of another gush of blood intensify her desire.

Yes, he's telling her he'll willingly bathe in this bright river of her red deeps, an illicit baptism, so he lays her down, tantalizes her to bring her to his own heat though she's already there, and his hands are imbrued. Her welling goes on over them both, bellies and legs. He loves the teeming of her girlish gore. Who would have thought the sweet girl had so much talent for blood? The sprinkled sheets become suffused, but who's to say that it's not his blood too? Actually, a lot of it is.

"Come, tell me, have all these annoying men— these clients—made you come?"

"No," she says, and she's sighing profoundly. "Not with any of those dumb stupid clients, only with myself and the other girls. We do each other when we feel like it."

"Well, you won't need to do yourself and each other quite so often, now that you have a man who will do you anytime you like."

"I never come with the men I have to do, I just pretend with them," she says.

"Well, you don't need to pretend, I'll take your rose nipples in my mouth and I've found your adorable button." And it's true, he has the most drifting feathering bloodstained fingers so that she's indeed gasping in the throes of her first pleasure with a man.

"You're so nice," says Rue. "And you taste good. Considering."

His breath tastes like plums, his body's got the rich blood-warm smell of a dark-haired man, like field-grown raspberries soaked in raspberry cordial. Mildly surprised, Rue thinks he means it, he wants me to come and she's climbing into a noonday zenith, already she's coming before he's well inside her, and, nearly weeping for wanting him, she arches her hips and pulls and sucks him in. Now she has his whole cock in her body and can grab on to the solid rest of her sweet, racing catastrophe. And like a stunning blow, he procures a spasm of violent pleasure, to be wondered at in view of his recently near-dead condition, the way he arrived at this place.

In a lull for breath, Rue finally asks Axior, "How come you know so much about love when you came from the other side of the mirror, and maybe the moon?"

"Because that knowledge always existed.

Everything exists," he says. "It's there already, all the reality and unreality, waiting for us to know it, feel it, and experience it. The way we're doing it now."

"Oh, I see what you mean."

"And my dearest Rue, your first coming was always there, but you had to wait to realize it. The same is true for me, when my endless existence meant nothing. Because endless existence has no passionate reality."

Rue twines her arms around him. "I like it when something makes perfect sense."

Between his blood and hers, the pillows are reddened, the sheets drenched to the mattress, the very walls finely flecked with pink and red wine, the spatter patterns circular and fan-shaped as in scenes of murders. A lot of the blood has got to be his, thinks Axior. His face drips, his head hurts badly where the wound has reopened.

Rue sits up. She likes looking at him. He's tired now. Bruised eyes black as sea almonds. She touches his hair that falls in dampish strands, straight and thick and black, oiled silk, spilling black light into her open palms.

"Let's run some water." she says, and slips naked into the bathroom to turn on the tap full force. "Cold is best," she says. "For blood."

She comes back for him. "We're such a mess," she happily says. "You're pretty hideous!" Her beloved is a red devil with glowing burgundy eyes, tender and horrifying with his black hair matted and disheveled. "You do look like a vampyre. Like a monster."

"As bad as that!" He seizes one of the thick white towels from the rack and wipes his body and hers, smirching its beautifully laundered whiteness.

Everything Axior does makes Rue laugh delightedly.

"Seraphita will have a fit when she sees the towels."

Axior picks her up in his arms. Their faces, shoulders, and bellies are still dappled and smeared, forearms streaked to the elbow and shoulder, hands and fingers daubed. "I suppose I must be pretty much of a ghoulish terror," Axior says, "while you are merely a blushing rosebud all over."

"Thank you!" says Rue. Tightening her arms around his neck, she looks at herself in the mirror. Her hair is pink worms, face newborn as a red babe from the womb. She squeals charmingly at the sight. "What about the iodine?" She lets herself down and opens the cabinet. The shelves are crammed with vaginal pharmacopoeia, ointments, pessaries, powders, and douches. Everything tumbles into the basin.

"I guess I don't have any first aid," says she.

"Don't bother. These are only scratches," he says after a quick scan. "They'll heal overnight. That's enough of washing and first aid. Let's have supper. It's here, though I didn't hear anybody coming in, did you?"

She shrugs mischievously. "It's the little banquet I ordered. Olga must have brought it in. She probably got an eyeful of us thrashing around." A tray has magically appeared on Rue's chaise longue of sky-blue velvet. The food is served on Limoges dishes painted with blue daisies.

They tear apart a cold roast fowl, devour a crusty loaf and a corner of brie and fresh peaches. They drink the whole bottle of red syrah and consume half a dark, moist cake baked with brandy and glacéed fruits. Strong French coffee, black. Axior produces cigarettes and finds he's acquired an instant taste for earthly food and smokes.

"This is very good," he says. "But come, Rue." He leads her to the bed. "We aren't tired yet. This is our wedding night."

He can't get enough of her, she can't get enough of him. They grow sodden with love. The girlish room, at one time Rue's nursery, is a scene of jubilant carnage. The reek of the bedchamber is as crimson and spiky as crushed geraniums. The night vibrates with consequence. Rue sleeps the rest of the night at last in Axior's arms.

He whispers in her ear about leaving her for a

while, but she barely hears him. By daybreak he's gone, vanished, though it can't be said without a trace because of the spatter patterns of the bedroom. Rue sits thoughtfully and struggles against feeling bereft. He can't mean to have left her. Not after this wedding orgy they've had together.

♦

In the morning, Madame Seraphita comes into Rue's room to examine the damage.

Shrill with indignation, she laments the state of the sheets and towels. She's like a committee of matrons after a wedding night, where it's the custom to flaunt the bride's virginity by draping the hymeneal linen from the window. But Madame's not bragging. She'll sue. But whom will she sue?

"This is *too much*. These sheets will have to be burned!" she cries out shocked, even though she was paid well enough to refurbish every bed in the house. Afterward, she changes her mind about the burning, for though Madame Seraphita is rich she's thrifty. She orders the maids to scrub and strip the room, launder and bleach the sheets and hang them to dry in the attic, after which they will be torn into dustcloths.

At nine in the morning, two Bell Telephone technicians arrive with a beautiful new instrument of bronze and ivory, a replica of the one Axior shot the night before. The men hook it up so that

Madame Seraphita doesn't have to lose a single hour of business. By ten, a linen company Madame Seraphita has never heard of delivers a box of three dozen sheets, even though only two sheets and four pillowcases were ruined during the nocturnal debauch. Madame Seraphita scrutinizes the sheets. They're the highest-quality Egyptian cotton, so finely woven they shimmer like moonbeams. Madame never saw such sheets, even during her apprenticeship in Paris.

His strength replenished, Axior returns. He can pretty much do anything. With both arms he raises the fire escape to its old position, getting it mortared into place, and repairing the house back to its old solidity. He easily mounts the fire escape, climbing through Rue's window to reclaim Rue, who waits breathlessly and flies into his arms. She has breakfast waiting: fresh muffins, butter, and strong fragrant coffee. They just don't stop being hungry.

They hear Madame Seraphita's loud cries. The trouble is she's found starlike asterisks tattooed on her wrists. When she tries scrubbing them off, more stars appear, looping around her arms. Nothing gets rid of them. Supernaturally tattooed, they reappear on her shoulders. They're ineradicable. Seraphita knows what this means. She hates losing her loveliest, most saleable asset, assuming she could ever tame Rue to the life. But Madame

Seraphita is not stupid. To get rid of the disfiguring tattoos, she's got to get rid of the two vexatious lovers.

They're happy to go.

From the fire escape, Rue and Axior can see that the flood waters have receded from the city streets. They run down the clanging iron staircase, the fire escape mystically revamped and soldered to the walls. Rue takes only what she needs: a few gowns, a bag of her favorite books. Madame Seraphita's girls throw rice at the newlyweds.

Rue and Axior follow the paths of the renewed gardens, where the sick vegetation has miraculously sprung back to life overnight, flourishing and brilliant red, engorged with sap and blood. Rue tramples the scarlet tulips with her silver heels, crushing the red hellebores and pointy crimson petals of the Christmas cactus, defiantly early this year.

"We'll take the Pierce Arrow touring car," she tells Axior. It's parked in her grandmother's three-car garage, where Madame keeps her automobiles covered in all seasons with fleecy horse blankets that descend from a pulley device in the ceiling.

"You wouldn't know anything about driving, of course," says Rue, "so you can leave it to me."

"Driving?" Axior laughs, enchanted with his bride's endless vocabulary. "What's that? Wait, I'll get it in a minute."

She hops up on the car, perching on the hood and crossing her long, sweet legs. "Too bad you haven't got a camera."

"I do, actually," says Axior, for he knows that honeymooners must have cameras, and he can get anything. He takes her picture. "You look like a star, a movie star."

"Oh, Axior, you're getting silly. I'm going to drive. You look for the maps in the glove box, my darling. You can navigate us to a nice, small, green town. We're getting out of Chemical City forever."

With her new husband and his radiant strange eyes, his vigorous, unworldly body and its sublunar demands, starstruck Rue leaves her prison. Of how her life will be, Rue knows little, and is too young to suspect. But what does she care, and what will it matter?

END

www.ingramcontent.com/pod-product-compliance
Lightning Source LLC
Chambersburg PA
CBHW050903120626
46554CB00003B/994